US IMMIGRATION AND CUSTOMS ENFORCEMENT

BY CYNTHIA KENNEDY HENZEL

CONTENT CONSULTANT

Luis F. Jiménez
Associate Professor of Political Science
University of Massachusetts Boston

Essential Library

An Imprint of Abdo Publishing | abdobooks.com

abdobooks.com

Published by Abdo Publishing, a division of ABDO, PO Box 398166, Minneapolis, Minnesota 55439. Copyright © 2021 by Abdo Consulting Group, Inc. International copyrights reserved in all countries. No part of this book may be reproduced in any form without written permission from the publisher. Essential Library™ is a trademark and logo of Abdo Publishing.

Printed in the United States of America, North Mankato, Minnesota.
102020
012021

THIS BOOK CONTAINS RECYCLED MATERIALS

Cover Photo: John Moore/Getty Images News/Getty Images
Interior Photos: Zack Frank/Shutterstock Images, 4–5; Eric Gay/AP Images, 6; Graeme Sloan/Sipa USA/AP Images, 12; Mary Altaffer/AP Images, 15; Diane Bondareff/AP Images, 16–17; Charles Dharapak/AP Images, 19; Gregory Bull/AP Images, 23; US Immigration and Customs Enforcement, 26–27, 30, 32, 34–35, 39, 46, 63, 74, 83, 92–93, 95; Greg L. Davis/US Customs and Border Protection, 40; Ed Andrieski/AP Images, 43; Tim Sloan/AP Images, 44–45; Wilfredo Lee/AP Images, 51; Red Line Editorial, 57; Evan Vucci/AP Images, 58–59, 68–69; Matt York/AP Images, 67, 77; John Moore/Getty Images News/Getty Images, 70–71; David Peinado/Pacific Press/Sipa USA/AP Images, 80–81; Ronen Tivony/SIPA USA/AP Images, 87; Tom Williams/CQ Roll Call/AP Images, 90

Editor: Charly Haley
Series Designer: Maggie Villaume

Library of Congress Control Number: 2020940282

Publisher's Cataloging-in-Publication Data

Names: Henzel, Cynthia Kennedy, author.
Title: US immigration and customs enforcement / by Cynthia Kennedy Henzel
Description: Minneapolis, Minnesota : Abdo Publishing, 2021 | Series: Special reports
    | Includes online resources and index
Identifiers: ISBN 9781532194160 (lib. bdg.) | ISBN 9781098213527 (ebook)
Subjects: LCSH: Immigration enforcement--United States--Juvenile literature. |
    United States--Emigration and immigration--History--Juvenile literature. |
    Immigration courts--Juvenile literature. | Deportation--United States--Juvenile
    literature. | Detention of persons--United States--Juvenile literature.
Classification: DDC 325.73--dc23

CONTENTS

CHAPTER ONE

THE
ENFORCER

Kevin Euceda and his sister wandered aimlessly through the Texas underbrush in 2017. They had traveled three months from Honduras to the border between Mexico and the United States. They had then floated on an inflatable raft across the Rio Grande, a river that forms part of that border, into Texas. They were hungry, tired, sick, and lost. But they had finally made it to the United States.

The US Border Patrol found them the next day and arrested them for entering the country illegally. Kevin's sister was 18 years old, so she was taken to a US Immigration and Customs Enforcement (ICE) detention center to await deportation, which is the removal of a person from a country. Kevin was only 17. Because he

Much of the border between Mexico and the United States is made up of harsh, rugged landscapes.

was a minor, the Border Patrol transferred him to the Office of Refugee Resettlement. This is the federal agency responsible for undocumented immigrant children who are found crossing the border alone or who are separated from their families. Kevin had no idea when he would see his sister again.

In 1997, a settlement from the US Supreme Court case *Flores v. Reno* required federal immigration authorities to maintain certain standards of care for undocumented immigrant children. This became known as the Flores Settlement. Because of these rules, the Office of Refugee

Families seeking asylum walk through an ICE detention center in Texas.

Resettlement gave Kevin clean clothes and food.

Kevin spoke with a therapist, Leyanira Trevino, who assured him that whatever he said was confidential. Kevin told Trevino about how he had come to seek asylum as a refugee in the United States. After his parents died when he was very young, he had lived with an abusive, alcoholic grandmother. She died when Kevin was 12, and MS-13, a violent gang, took their house. Having nowhere else to go, Kevin worked for the gang, first running errands and then selling drugs.

REFUGEES AND ASYLEES

People who are fleeing violence or persecution in their own countries are considered separate from those immigrating for economic or family reasons, and different rules apply to them. Those who are fleeing are divided into two groups: refugees and asylees. Refugees are people who apply for entry into the United States from another country to avoid persecution for ethnic, religious, or other reasons. The president, with the approval of the US Congress, decides each year how many refugees the United States will accept. Asylees are also people fleeing persecution. However, asylees are people who apply to stay in the United States from a US port of entry or who apply after less than a year in the country as an undocumented immigrant. There is no limit on the number of asylees who may be accepted, so the United States can't turn back people from the border because there are too many. However, the United States can deny entry to asylees after processing their applications.

The young teenager had witnessed torture and murder. He had even kicked his cousin as the boy was beaten by MS-13 members for refusing to join the gang. Ashamed, Kevin had snuck out of the house shortly afterward, but the gunshots he heard left no doubt about his cousin's fate. Kevin was then told that to stay in the gang, he had to kill a stranger. Kevin did not want to do this. He talked his sister into helping him flee to the United States. As they traveled north from Honduras, Kevin received constant threatening messages from members of MS-13. They said they would kill him if they caught him.

IN CUSTODY

Under the Flores Settlement rules, Kevin would have been held less than 20 days before being released to family or a guardian while he waited for a court decision on whether the United States would accept him as a refugee. However, the rules changed under President Donald Trump's administration. Kevin was not released. Trevino, the therapist, was required to turn over her notes to the Department of Health and Human Services (HHS). Unknown to Kevin or Trevino, HHS shared notes with ICE when children mentioned gang affiliations. By telling Trevino the truth, Kevin had given ICE reason to detain him while he waited on his court date. ICE determined he might be dangerous and moved him in shackles to Shenandoah Valley Juvenile Center in Virginia, a high-security juvenile detention center, where juveniles who had been convicted of crimes were held.

As months passed, Kevin became depressed. He had a new counselor, Andrew Mayles, but Kevin didn't trust him. Still, Mayles worked to help Kevin. He eventually got Kevin accepted by the government's antitrafficking program as a victim of human trafficking because he had been forced to work with MS-13. People fleeing human trafficking can get refugee status.

After 170 days in custody, Kevin turned 18. In the past, undocumented children were often released to take care of themselves after turning 18 because they were considered adults. They were expected to voluntarily show up for

MS-13

One of the priorities of ICE has been targeting violent street gangs like MS-13. This gang was established in Los Angeles, California, in the 1970s and spread to El Salvador through deportation of gang members from the United States. It is suspected to be part of major drug operations, smuggling, and human trafficking, as well as murders and other violent crimes. ICE raids, such as Operation Matador in 2017, arrest hundreds of suspected gang members. The people who are arrested during the raids can be charged with illegal entry into the United States by ICE even if they cannot be charged with another crime by local authorities. Possible participation in the gang can be used in immigration court as a reason to hold suspects in detention rather than release them on bond. In 2019, ICE gang investigations resulted in seizures of 820 firearms and 5,500 pounds (2,495 kg) of illegal drugs.[1]

court dates. But after the rule changes under the Trump administration, ICE could use Kevin's therapy notes as justification to hold him. ICE moved Kevin to a detention center for adults. Kevin was scared. He slept in a room with a hundred other men. The lights were always on. There was no privacy. Here, he had a new therapist. Although Kevin was cautious about what he said now, he admitted to getting angry when other inmates picked on him. He told his therapist that he felt like "he was going to explode."[2] These notes again went to ICE.

After another five months, Kevin had a court hearing to decide whether he could be released on bond while he waited on the court's asylum decision. He watched on a TV screen from a cell as his volunteer student lawyers made his case. Judge Helaine R. Perlman of the Arlington Immigration Court ordered Kevin released. It had been 329 days since he had been arrested. But Kevin's saga was not over. ICE filed an appeal, and Kevin went back to his cell. Six months later, Judge Perlman granted Kevin asylum.

"SOMETIMES I DON'T LIKE TO TALK ABOUT [MY PLANS], IN CASE THEY DON'T HAPPEN. BUT I KNOW THERE ARE BIG OPPORTUNITIES HERE [IN THE UNITED STATES]."[3]

—KEVIN EUCEDA, ICE DETAINEE

MORE TO THE
STORY

SHARING INFORMATION

The Office of Refugee Resettlement signed an agreement with ICE in April 2018 to formally share information about children in custody. The government declared this was proper because the Office of Refugee Resettlement acts as the guardian of the children in its care and can therefore decide whether to share information. In addition, the Office of Refugee Resettlement signed an agreement to "develop additional information" about the children during their weekly therapy sessions.[4] ICE regulations gave therapists two additional requirements. First, children must be informed that they should be honest but that information they disclose could affect their release. Second, if a child mentions gangs or drug dealing, therapists must file a report to ICE within four hours. Many therapists did not agree with the policy; some even kept two sets of notes so they could keep incriminating information from ICE. On February 17, 2020, the American Psychological Association denounced the practice of using therapists' notes to target immigrant children. After public outcry about Kevin Euceda's case, on March 4, 2020, the US Congress introduced bills in both the House and Senate that would deny ICE the right to use therapists' notes against child immigrants. Secretary of HHS Alex Azar told members of Congress that his agency had stopped turning over these records.

Again, ICE filed an appeal. Kevin remained in custody as the appeal process moved forward.

WHAT IS ICE?

ICE is an agency within the US Department of Homeland Security (DHS). It is responsible for enforcing approximately 400 federal immigration laws. ICE also enforces labor laws regarding undocumented immigrants working in the United States.

ICE investigates crimes such as smuggling, illegal employment of undocumented immigrants, money laundering, human trafficking, and entering the country illegally. ICE can arrest people, including those whose only crime is crossing the border illegally. The agency

ICE is headquartered in Washington, DC.

detains immigrants arrested by ICE officers as well as those apprehended by US Border and Customs Protection for illegal entry into the United States. ICE runs many detention facilities to hold these detainees until a US immigration court decides whether they will be deported.

ICE employs its own attorneys. They represent the US government as prosecutors in trials in the immigration courts. If the court decides an immigrant will be deported, ICE is responsible for removing the person from the country.

THE IMMIGRANT POPULATION

ICE has a huge job. According to Pew Research Center, about 10.5 million undocumented immigrants lived in the United States in 2017.[5] This number

IMMIGRATION LAW

The Immigration and Nationality Act provides the laws for immigration into the United States. The priorities for allowing immigration under the law are to unify families, increase the number of workers with needed skills, protect refugees, and promote diversity. US law allows 675,000 visas for permanent residency each year, plus visas for spouses, parents, and children of US citizens younger than 21. Other family members such as siblings or grandparents can get visas under the preferred family program, although it may take decades. Refugees are not counted in this number. The diversity requirement limits the number of immigrants from one country that can get visas. Only 7 percent of people immigrating in one year can come from a single country.[6] This means that people in countries where many people wish to immigrate to the United States—such as Mexico, India, and China—must wait longer than people from other countries.

changes constantly as some are deported or leave and others arrive.

Undocumented immigrants cover a wide range of people in the United States. Some people have lived in the country for years, marrying and raising their families in the United States. Some are migrant laborers who come to the country seasonally to work. Some are recent immigrants seeking employment and a better life for their children. Some are people who were brought to the United States as children and know nothing about their country of birth. Some arrived legally with a visa but stayed after their visa expired. A relatively small number are criminals: smugglers, human traffickers, gang members, terrorists, or others.

Legal immigration to the United States is a long process. There are strict quotas on how many immigrants are allowed into the country. There are also preferences for immigrants with family already in the United States or who have specific job skills. This means many people have little chance to immigrate to the United States.

According to Pew Research Center, undocumented immigrants represent about 5 percent of the US workforce.

For many immigrants, their ultimate goal is to become US citizens, a process that can be long and arduous.

In 2014, they did 26 percent of US farming jobs.[7] They are also heavily represented in construction, factory work, and service work in hotels and restaurants.

Some people believe it would be impossible or problematic to deport all undocumented immigrants. They believe laws should change to help undocumented people live and work in the United States legally. Others believe that the law is the law—if people are in the country illegally, they should be deported. It is ICE's job to carry out the shifting policies of immigration, including managing the millions of undocumented immigrants who are in the US immigration legal system. ICE is also responsible for protecting the United States from people who might cause harm from outside the country's borders.

CHAPTER TWO

THE ORIGIN
OF ICE

O n September 11, 2001, the United States suffered
a devastating terrorist attack. Nineteen terrorists
from al-Qaeda, an Islamic extremist group,
hijacked airplanes and crashed into buildings in New
York City and Washington, DC. The attack killed 2,977
people and injured thousands of others.[1] It also made
the United States realize how vulnerable it was to
terrorism and how unprepared the country was to
protect itself.

In response to the attack, President George W.
Bush reorganized parts of the US government that
were responsible for protecting the country. In 2002,
Congress passed the Homeland Security Act, which

In the aftermath of the September 11 terrorist attack, President Bush's
administration restructured national security, including the agencies
dealing with immigration law enforcement.

THE SEPTEMBER 11 ATTACK

On September 11, 2001, 19 extremists from the foreign terrorist group al-Qaeda hijacked four commercial airplanes using knives and box cutters as weapons. Hijackers flew two of the planes into the Twin Towers of the World Trade Center in New York City. The massive explosions and resulting fires caused the towers to collapse. Another plane hit the Pentagon, which is the headquarters for the US Department of Defense, near Washington, DC. Passengers on the fourth plane, who had learned about the fate of the other planes, fought back against the hijackers, leading to a crash in a field in Pennsylvania. On October 7, in response to the attack, the United States and its allies launched Operation Enduring Freedom against the Taliban, the ruling regime in Afghanistan that supported al-Qaeda leader Osama bin Laden. Although the Taliban quickly fell, the group fled to Pakistan and has resurged several times. On May 2, 2011, US military forces in Pakistan killed bin Laden.

created the US Department of Homeland Security (DHS). The mission of the new department was to counter terrorism and homeland security threats, protect US borders, secure critical infrastructure and cyberspace, and defend the nation's economy.

All or parts of 22 federal agencies and programs were either moved from other departments to become part of DHS or were dissolved and replaced by DHS. Among those dissolved was the Immigration and Naturalization Service (INS), which had been under the Department of Justice. The INS had been responsible for immigration applications, immigrant services, and enforcement of immigration policies. Other agencies absorbed by DHS included the

US Customs Service, which had been part of the US

Treasury, and the US Border Patrol, which had been part of

the Department of Labor.

DHS began operations in March 2003. It divided

the responsibilities of INS, the Customs Service, and the

Border Patrol between three new agencies. The first was

US Citizenship and Immigration Services (USCIS). That

agency is responsible for immigrant applications and

services. It is not a law enforcement agency. The second

was US Customs and Border Protection (CBP), which is

responsible for enforcing immigration laws at the 325 US

ports of entry.[2] It can detain, investigate, and arrest people

The first secretary of homeland security was
former Pennsylvania governor Tom Ridge.

suspected of breaking immigration laws while entering the United States. The US Border Patrol is a part of CBP and is responsible for monitoring the land borders of the United States. The Border Patrol can investigate, arrest, and detain undocumented immigrants within 99 miles (159 km) of US borders. The third new agency created as part of DHS was ICE.

FIRST DIRECTOR OF ICE

In 2003, President Bush appointed Michael J. Garcia the assistant secretary for Immigration and Customs Enforcement, making him the head of ICE. The Senate unanimously confirmed him. Garcia had previously served as the assistant secretary of commerce for export enforcement. He had also served as a federal attorney and prosecuted high-profile terrorist cases.

HOW ICE IS ORGANIZED

ICE is the second-largest federal law enforcement unit after the Federal Bureau of Investigation (FBI), with more than 20,000 law enforcement and support personnel. ICE has more than 400 offices in the United States and around the world.[3] The head of ICE is appointed by the president and must be approved by the Senate. ICE is divided into three sections that carry out the agency's missions: Homeland Security Investigations (HSI), Enforcement and Removal Operations (ERO), and the Office of the Principal Legal Advisor (OPLA).

The Management and Administration branch supports those three sections.

HSI investigates immigration crime, human smuggling, narcotics and weapons smuggling, financial crimes, and cybercrime. It has more than 6,500 special agents and 700 intelligence analysts.[4] It also conducts investigations to protect critical infrastructure and industries from sabotage, attack, or exploitation.

Within HSI, the Office of Intelligence collects, analyzes, and shares intelligence data with ICE and DHS officials. This includes data on people, money, and materials moving into, within, and out of the United States. Intelligence agents receive approximately 1,800 classified reports or messages each day.[5] Another part of HSI, the International Operations Division, works with international law enforcement agencies.

DETENTION AND REMOVAL

The second ICE section, ERO, is responsible for locating undocumented immigrants in the country and deporting them. They may do this through raids at homes or businesses. These raids often follow ICE intelligence investigations or tips from local law enforcement agencies. ICE officers also work with local jails to find undocumented people who have been accused or convicted of crimes.

In 2020, ICE had approximately 6,100 deportation officers.[6] They identify and arrest suspects and transport them to ICE detention facilities. They detain undocumented immigrants waiting on court hearings or supervise those who are out on bond or released under other alternatives to detention programs. Finally, if courts decide people must be deported, ICE removes those people from the country.

Officers in ERO may use ICE detainer requests to ask state or local law enforcement to hold people in jail after their release date who are suspected of being in the United States without permission. This includes people who have paid a bond for release, have been acquitted of a crime or had charges dismissed, or who have served their time in jail. Detainer requests allow ICE officers time to arrest undocumented

"MOST OF MY DAY IS SPENT OUT IN THE FIELD, LOCATING FUGITIVES WHO EITHER ARE CONVICTED CRIMINALS, SEXUAL OFFENDERS, GANG MEMBERS, MURDERERS."[7]

—AYEISHA RAMIREZ, ICE DEPORTATION OFFICER

immigrants who have been arrested by local authorities on suspicion of other crimes.

ICE's OPLA provides legal advice and represents the US government in federal courts. Its 1,100 attorneys are responsible for prosecuting cases regarding the removal of undocumented immigrants. In addition, OPLA provides legal advice to other departments concerning labor laws, ethics, contracts with ICE facilities and personnel, and other legal matters. This section also defends ICE authorities accused of wrongdoing in federal court.

ICE officers take a man into custody during a six-day nationwide immigration sweep.

THE IMMIGRANT JUDICIAL SYSTEM

Special immigration courts and judges hear immigration matters. These cases may involve refugees seeking asylum, people fighting deportation orders, or people attempting to stay in the country legally. Immigration courts and judges are not part of the federal court system, which is controlled by the judicial branch of government. They are part of the executive branch of government under the Department of Justice.

There are 67 US immigration courts and more than 450 immigration judges.[8] Each judge may be responsible for about 2,000 cases at any given time, which is double the caseload of federal district court judges.[9] The average wait time for hearing cases in immigration court is more than two years. In some parts of the country, it is almost four years. In October 2019, the immigration court system had a backlog of more than one million cases.

ICE is responsible for the thousands of people awaiting court hearings. Criminal offenses are not tried in immigration courts. So undocumented immigrants who have broken criminal laws may be tried in criminal courts and serve time in jail before facing immigration court.

People can appeal decisions made by the immigration court to the Board of Immigration Appeals. The board's 20 members decide approximately 30,000 appeals each year. Generally, the Board of Immigration Appeals grants a stay so the person cannot be deported while the court case is ongoing.

DIFFERENT RULES

The rules of immigration courts are different from those of other US courts. Undocumented immigrants are entitled to be tried in a court for crimes, including immigration offenses, under the 14th Amendment to the US Constitution. However, people in immigration court are not entitled to an attorney to represent them as they are in criminal court. They may hire an attorney, or they may get help from nonprofit organizations. Judges in immigration courts are not entirely independent, as other federal judges are. They are employees of the Department of Justice, which some people believe could make them less impartial than other federal judges.

The US attorney general can overrule decisions made by the Board of Immigration Appeals. Also, people have 30 days to appeal decisions by the Board of Immigration Appeals to the US Court of Appeals, part of the judicial branch. However, once the Board of Immigration Appeals has made a decision, the person loses protection from being deported. Unless granted another stay, a person may be deported before the case is accepted or decided by the US Court of Appeals.

CHAPTER THREE

INTERNATIONAL EFFORTS

As part of DHS, which the government created in the aftermath of the September 11 terrorist attack, ICE initially focused on helping defend the United States from international terrorism. Large terrorist and criminal organizations need a lot of money to fund their operations. ICE officials realized that one way to curtail terrorism was to follow the money. Early on, an ICE priority was to prevent terrorist organizations from receiving money they needed to support their people and operations. This led to efforts to combat international money laundering, smuggling, and human trafficking.

In 2003, ICE launched Operation Cornerstone to disrupt the financial dealings of criminals moving

Specially trained and equipped ICE teams deal with particularly risky situations, including those involving violent gangs and terrorism.

money into and out of the country. ICE agents worked with banks and other financial entities to curb criminal exploitation of their systems. ICE also participated in the El Dorado Task Force, which brought together local, state, and federal law enforcement agencies to root out money laundering. Money laundering is the way that criminals disguise the origins of money made illegally—such as cash from selling drugs—by passing it through banks or shell companies.

Another way international criminals move money is through the global trade system. They hide money by falsifying invoices and documents and by moving illegal goods through the system. These schemes provide

PROTECTING WEAPONS

The ICE Arms and Strategic Technology Investigations Unit is responsible for preventing terrorist groups and other enemies from getting military weapons and sensitive technology. ICE officers recover weapons and arrest arms dealers. In 2005, ICE prevented the smuggling of AK-47 assault rifles to terrorists in Colombia. ICE agents have prevented smuggling of aircraft and fighter jet components to Iran, China, Thailand, and Indonesia. In addition, ICE indicted Humayun Khan for smuggling components of nuclear weapons to Pakistan. His partner, Asher Kami, pleaded guilty to exporting components to India for use in its missile and nuclear program. Other technology ICE has prevented from falling into enemy hands includes laser sights, night vision technology, and experimental aircraft. ICE also maintains an industry outreach program, Project Shield America, to work with US industries and exporters to prevent the illegal exportation of conventional weapons, technology, and chemical and biological weapons.

billions of illegal dollars to criminals each year. The ICE Trade Transparency Unit gathers information and works with other countries to make trade more transparent. The unit has developed a computer system that allows both countries in a trade exchange to see information from both sides of the transaction. This lets agents find discrepancies that lead to discoveries of illegal activity.

SMUGGLING

ICE works with CBP to catch people who attempt to avoid paying taxes on items brought into the United States. One way these smugglers avoid paying to import merchandise is through the in-bond system. This system allows people to move goods through the United States that are not intended for the US market. Smugglers might avoid paying customs charges by claiming goods were exported when they were not. They also might remove goods from a ship between ports.

"EVERY DAY, CARGO CONTAINERS CONTAINING BILLIONS OF DOLLARS' WORTH OF COUNTERFEIT GOODS ENTER THE UNITED STATES THROUGH ITS LAND, SEA, AND AIRPORTS OF ENTRY."[1]

—STEVE FRANCIS, DIRECTOR OF THE INTELLECTUAL PROPERTY RIGHTS CENTER, PART OF HSI

Another of ICE's missions is to disrupt the smuggling of counterfeit merchandise. The United States protects inventors, entrepreneurs, and companies by allowing them to patent new inventions and trademark intellectual property. According to the International Anti-Counterfeiting Coalition, theft of intellectual property costs US businesses several hundred billion dollars per year.

ICE has run countless operations to stop this theft. In June 2018, ICE agents seized 181,615 counterfeit items at the US–Mexico border in Laredo, Texas. The falsified brands found in the 795 boxes included Apple, Adidas, Coach, Marvel Comics, Nike, Samsung, and Hugo Boss,

Inspecting international cargo is part of ICE's anti-smuggling efforts.

along with other well-known clothing, cosmetic, and electronics brands. The merchandise had a street value of $42.9 million. The merchandise had come from China and was being exported to Mexico. It would have been sold in Mexico, and the profits would have helped fund a large criminal enterprise. ICE identified the cartel attempting to move the goods as the same one from which ICE had seized $16.1 million in merchandise the month before.[2] In February 2020, ICE in conjunction with other federal agencies seized 176,000 fake Super Bowl items such as jerseys, jewelry, and hats. If sold as authentic, the merchandise would have been worth $123 million.[3]

HUMAN TRAFFICKING

ICE has also seen success in fighting against human trafficking. Human trafficking

HUMAN SMUGGLING

Human smuggling is different from human trafficking. Human smuggling involves consenting people who pay to be smuggled across a border. Once across the border, human smugglers leave their clients on their own. Those who smuggle people from Mexico across the border into the United States are called coyotes. Coyotes may bring people across the border on foot or smuggle them in trucks. Traveling with a coyote can be dangerous. Some coyote clients die in the deserts, are trapped in hot trucks, or drown trying to cross the Rio Grande. In a report produced for the Department of Homeland Security in 2019, border crossers from Mexico paid anywhere from $6,000 to $10,000 to be smuggled into the United States.[4]

ICE agents carried out an anti-human trafficking operation at a Texas nightclub in 2017.

is the illegal process of transporting people against their will, often to be sold for forced labor or sexual exploitation. Human trafficking generates $32 billion per year and provides funds for criminals around the world.[5] Approximately 50,000 people are trafficked into the United States each year. More than half of these cases in 2018 involved child victims of sex trafficking.[6]

In 2003, ICE launched Operation Predator to protect children, including those who were being trafficked, from sexual predators. Many trafficking crimes depend on the internet to find and sell victims. In 2009, the ICE Cyber Crimes Center opened an investigation called Operation

Delego. It discovered an international online forum for the distribution of child pornography. Of the 600 members identified, 70 were indicted.[7] Through Operation Predator, and working with multiple agencies in the United States and foreign law enforcement agencies, ICE agents arrested 8,000 child predators by 2012.[8] In addition, ICE works to protect children who are exploited over the internet.

Human trafficking has continued to be a priority for ICE. In 2019, ICE investigators began 1,024 investigations related to human trafficking. They arrested 2,197 people, criminally charged 1,113, and convicted 691. They identified and helped 428 victims.[9]

CYBERCRIMES

ICE Cyber Crimes Center provides technical services for investigations into cross-border crime. Within the Cyber Crimes Center is the Cyber Crimes Unit, the Child Exploitation Investigations Unit, and the Computer Forensics Unit. The Cyber Crimes Unit investigates online criminal activity. The Forensics Unit specializes in recovering digital evidence. Forensics analysts examine computer drives, cell phones, and other devices and provide evidence in court. The Child Exploitation Investigations Unit works to halt exploitation of children. In 2018, ICE Cyber Crimes Center processed more than 7,300 terabytes (or 7.3 petabytes) of data. One petabyte is equivalent to 65 copies of the entire Library of Congress.[10]

In addition to arresting child predators, ICE has worked to help children and adults avoid becoming victims. In 2013, it launched a smartphone app that lets users see alerts about wanted child predators and report those suspected of a crime. In 2014, it launched Project iGuardian as part of the national cybersafety campaign to protect kids from online predators.

CHAPTER FOUR

IMMIGRATION
ENFORCEMENT

In addition to thwarting the illegal movement of money, goods, and people across US borders, ICE is tasked with removing undocumented immigrants. In 2003, ICE Detention and Removal Operations (now known as the Enforcement and Removal Operations) established eight Fugitive Operations Teams to carry out this mission. They arrested 1,900 people in 2003.[1] In 2004, ICE added an additional ten Fugitive Operations Teams. With the increasing number of immigrants arrested, detention of people as they awaited court hearings became a problem. ICE established an alternative-to-detention program commonly known as "catch and release," to alleviate the issue. Immigrants who were not considered a danger to the public could

ICE officers carry out an enforcement operation in 2017.

remain with their families or in their communities as they waited on the courts to hear their cases. ICE added 26 more teams in 2005, resulting in the arrest of 7,959 undocumented immigrants that year.[2]

Since the primary purpose of Detention and Removal Operations was to remove undocumented immigrants involved in criminal behavior, a new program called Operation Community Shield began in 2005. Community Shield targeted undocumented immigrants involved in criminal gangs such as MS-13. These gangs are responsible for much of the illegal drug distribution in the United States.

287(g)

ICE recognized the need to work with local communities to identify undocumented immigrants who were involved in criminal activity. The Illegal Immigration Reform and Immigrant Responsibility Act, passed in 1996, had a section called 287(g). That section allowed local law enforcement to screen people in jails for immigration violations. In 2006, a sheriff in North Carolina, Jim Pendergraph, let his deputies screen the general population for immigration violations. Seeing a good opportunity, ICE expanded the program. Through the 287(g) program, some state and local law enforcement agencies signed agreements with DHS to authorize state and local officers to perform the functions of federal immigration agents under the supervision of ICE.

The increased number of ICE officers plus the cooperation of state and local law enforcement officers resulted in the arrest of even more undocumented immigrants, reducing the number of fugitive cases. In October 2007, ICE had approximately 595,000 cases of fugitive undocumented immigrants. This was 38,000 fewer than just a year before.[3]

However, a November 2006 report showed that ICE

ICE 287(g) TRAINING

State and local law enforcement officers officially working with ICE through 287(g) receive training in how to access immigrations databases, fill out immigration forms, and other federal immigration agent responsibilities. They also receive some training on civil rights and community outreach. As of March 2017, ICE had trained and certified more than 1,822 police officers to act as immigration enforcement agents. Some were authorized to interrogate and arrest suspected undocumented immigrants.

They trained for four weeks at the Federal Law Enforcement Training Center ICE Academy in Charleston, South Carolina. As of 2020, these trainings had been discontinued. ICE no longer lets local police arrest suspected undocumented immigrants on their own after ICE began to receive bad publicity about 287(g) enforcements. Local police still work with ICE as warrant service officers, meaning they can arrest suspects with warrants issued by ICE. Warrant service officers go through a one-day training by ICE instructors, which may be done online or locally.

was having problems tracking its detainees. ICE officers were not inputting information into computer systems quickly enough, making it hard for families to locate their loved ones who had been detained. Because records were not updated, ICE was paying detention centers to hold detainees who had actually been released.

NUMBERS GAME

ICE's work was not the only reason that the number of undocumented immigrant deportations increased in the early 2000s. Another reason was a change in how the government counted the number of deportations. Previously, most people caught crossing the US–Mexico border illegally were loaded onto buses and sent back to Mexico as what was called *voluntary returns* or *returns*. These people, numbering more than one million a

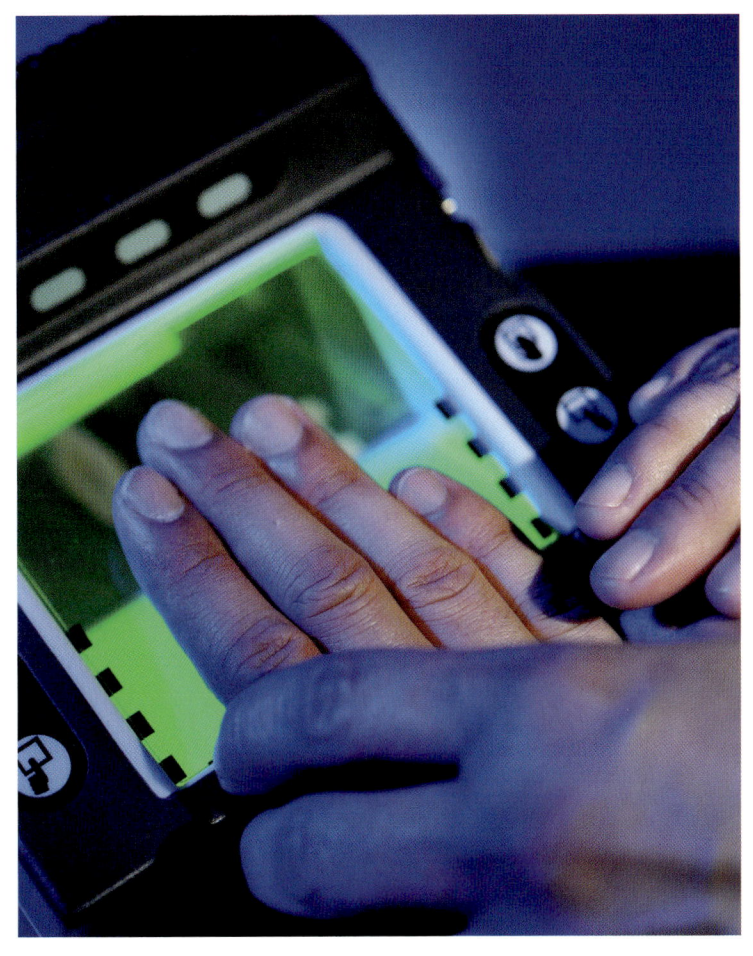

ICE gathers fingerprints from the people it detains in order to build a record for use in future enforcement.

year, were not counted in the official government deportation statistics.

Under President George W. Bush's administration, this policy changed. Those caught illegally crossing the border were now fingerprinted and formally deported. This ensured that the government had a record of these

CBP agents work to apprehend people along the border between the United States and Mexico.

undocumented immigrants. These actions were termed *removals*. The consequences of removals were greater than for those of returns because the US government keeps records of people who are deported. Illegally entering the United States after being deported is considered a more serious crime than illegally entering for the first time.

With this policy change, the increase in deportations was mostly a result of people captured within 100 miles (161 km) of the US–Mexico border. These immigrants were arrested by CBP, but they went into the ICE system, as ICE was responsible for all deportations.

LABOR TARGETED

Many undocumented immigrants come to the United States to find work. They supply labor to industries that may otherwise be short on workers due to low pay. These industries include agriculture, meat processing, hotels and restaurants, and construction. US law makes it illegal for businesses to hire workers who are undocumented. However, many businesses choose to ignore the law.

ICE periodically raids businesses suspected of having unauthorized workers. The business owners are fined, and the workers are deported. In Operation Wagon Train in December 2006, ICE agents raided several Swift meat-processing plants in six states. They arrested 1,300 undocumented immigrants who worked at the plants.[4] As word spread of the raid in Greeley, Colorado, protesters flocked to the plant.

"EVERYONE ON THE PRODUCTION FLOOR WAS SHOUTING, 'LA MIGRA! LA MIGRA!' THERE WERE PEOPLE HIDING BEHIND MACHINERY, IN BOXES, EVEN IN THE CARCASSES."[5]

—MONICA LOYA, FORMER SWIFT PLANT WORKER

LABOR SHORTAGES

Finding people to do the jobs often done by undocumented immigrants can be difficult. After the raids that hit Swift meatpacking plants in 2006, the tiny town of Cactus, Texas, lost 300 residents, about 10 percent of the town. Swift eventually recovered, although not by hiring US citizens. The new Brazilian owners of the plant paid slightly higher wages and replaced the workers with refugees from Thailand, Malaysia, Sudan, Somalia, and other countries. A local man, Stan Corbin, worked with the refugees to help them learn English and navigate US culture, from using indoor plumbing to getting drivers' licenses. "What we need is people willing to work hard," says Corbin. "Their children will grow up to be engineers. But right now in our country, there is a great need for laborers."[8]

The arrested immigrants were put into six large buses and several vans and taken to an ICE holding facility.

Under President Barack Obama, who took office after President Bush, there were fewer workplace raids. However, ICE workplace raids increased again under Obama's successor, President Donald Trump. By July 2018, ICE had sent out more than 5,200 notices to businesses that their records would be checked.[6] ICE raided seven chicken-processing plants in Mississippi in 2019 and arrested 680 undocumented immigrants.[7]

A crowd of protesters gathered outside the Swift plant in Greeley, Colorado, during the ICE raid.

CHAPTER FIVE

CHANGING
PRIORITIES

A s President Obama took office in 2009 amid an economic downturn, the number of immigrants crossing the border slowed. However, Obama continued many Bush immigration policies, and he implemented new policies to increase deportations. The Secure Communities program, created in 2008, began to help ICE track undocumented immigrants. Under Secure Communities, if people were arrested, their fingerprints could be run against not only criminal databases but also immigration databases. If these people were in the immigration database, ICE could issue a detainer so they would remain in jail until ICE picked them up. President Obama suspended the

Under the Obama administration, some ICE programs continued as they had before, and others changed.

program in 2014, but President Trump reactivated it in 2017.

Obama also continued a process called expedited removal that allowed CBP officials to deport immigrants without going through the immigration deportation process. However, expedited removal allowed Border Patrol officers to deport noncitizens only if they were

Controversy has arisen over who has been detained in ICE's detention centers.

caught within two weeks of arrival and within 100 miles (161 km) of the border.

THE BED QUOTA

In 2009, conservative members of Congress passed a law that required ICE to maintain detention beds for 34,000 people. This so-called "bed quota" was to encourage ICE to detain more undocumented immigrants rather than release them to await court hearings. In 2010, funding for DHS was tied to fulfilling the bed quota. Although some proponents of the quota maintained that the new law did not require ICE to detain 34,000 people, it was generally understood that these beds were not built to sit empty.[1] ICE did not have the workers or budget to build detention facilities for 34,000 people, so it contracted with companies that specialized in detention. By 2015, private prisons operated 90 percent of detention centers for ICE detainees.[2]

Even though illegal immigration to the United States had slowed after the crash of the economy in 2008, ICE still found people to fill the beds. ICE expanded the number of undocumented immigrants it arrested who had been stopped by local officials under the 287(g) program. ICE also arrested legal residents, such as green card holders, who had committed crimes that might result in deportation.

In 2009, ICE began a series of raids called Operation Cross Check to remove undocumented immigrants. The program targeted those convicted of crimes. Over the next two years, seven regional and two national Operation Cross Check raids arrested 7,400 undocumented felons.[3]

PRIVATE DETENTION

In 2018, more than 70 percent of immigrant detainees were in facilities operated by private companies.[4] Two companies, CoreCivic and GEO Group, managed more than half the private prisons in the country. These contractors are paid by the bed; beds that are not used on a given day do not earn money for the company. ICE paid about $126 per bed in 2018.[5] The companies spend millions of lobbying dollars each year to influence Congress to adopt policies that favor incarceration because the more people who are detained, the higher their profits will be.

PROSECUTORIAL DISCRETION

In 2011, ICE director John Morton issued a new policy called prosecutorial discretion to try to return ICE to its original mission of targeting dangerous criminals by reducing the detention and deportation of people not considered a danger to the

MORE TO THE STORY

TARGETING LEGAL RESIDENTS

In two separate cases in 2014, ICE picked up men who were not US citizens but were legal permanent residents of the United States. Mark, from South Korea, and Richard, from Jamaica, had both immigrated as children. While growing up in the United States, both men had committed crimes that negated their legal status. According to a 1996 law that was seldom enforced, people convicted of a felony, a serious misdemeanor, or three minor misdemeanors could lose their right to legal-residency status. As a teenager, Mark had been convicted for possession of a small amount of marijuana. Richard had a conviction stemming from a schoolyard fight in high school. Fifteen years later, they both had steady jobs and families and had not been in trouble since their convictions. Suddenly, ICE officials came to their homes, and they were both arrested. They were both sent to detention facilities to await a decision by the immigration court on whether they would be deported. Six months later, Mark was released on bond. He lived in California, where the Ninth Circuit Court had ruled that people could not be detained for more than six months without a bond hearing. Richard, who lived on the East Coast, waited in detention over two years before a hearing.

community. This prosecutorial discretion allowed ICE officers to decide whether to issue or cancel a detainer request or a Notice to Appear before the immigration court. Officers had more leniency in decisions regarding whom to stop and question and whom to arrest. They were also encouraged to use other forms of deportation, such as expedited removal, instead of clogging the immigration courts.

This gave a massive amount of authority to ICE officers in the field, and it was not always welcomed by the officers. In 2011, Morton told agents to focus on immigration violators who posed the greatest threat to US security. With so many deportations, it was difficult for ICE officers to make determinations about the people they were tasked with arresting. One officer said in *Quartz* news magazine, "If I decide not to arrest someone [who is] here illegally, and they kill someone, then what?"[6]

In 2012, ICE added more Fugitive Operations Teams, increasing the total number of teams to 129.[7] A nationwide Operation Cross Check in 2012 arrested 3,168 undocumented immigrants in six days. This included 1,063 people convicted of felonies and 698 convicted criminals

John Morton served as the director of ICE from 2009 until 2013.

who had received deportation orders but remained in the country. Those arrested also included 559 people who had been deported from the country and returned.[8] This crime has a penalty of up to 20 years in prison.

Altogether, the teams arrested 37,371 people in 2012, their largest number in a single year. In 2013, ICE deported 438,000 people, a record for a single year. Expedited removals accounted for 43 percent of this number.[9]

BACKLASH

The huge number of undocumented immigrants caught in the system led to many problems. Detention centers were crowded, and living conditions inside them were poor. Communities were becoming upset as large numbers of undocumented immigrants who had committed no crimes disappeared into the system. The American Civil Liberties Union (ACLU), a civil rights advocacy organization, filed lawsuits for problems including inhumane conditions in detention facilities, unfair removal by expedited deportation, and unwarranted detention.

Tensions surrounding ICE increased in 2014, when large numbers of unaccompanied immigrant children arrived at the US–Mexico border from Honduras, El Salvador, and Guatemala, known as the Northern Triangle countries. Photos appeared of children kept in fenced enclosures as they awaited processing by CBP. According to the 1997 Flores Settlement, children could only be detained 20 days before release to family or guardians. This became impossible in 2014 as 68,541 unaccompanied children arrived at the US border, overwhelming the system.[10]

Generally, detained families were kept together in facilities or released into the community to await court hearings. Obama had ended family detentions in 2009. But as more and more immigrants arrived at the border, he revised the policy, hoping to discourage families from arriving in more numbers than the system could process.

DACA

One of the groups of undocumented immigrants Obama did not want targeted was people who had been brought to the United States as children.

In June 2012, Secretary of Homeland Security Janet Napolitano issued a statement on prosecutorial discretion involving this group of people. This program, which came to be called Deferred Action for Childhood Arrivals (DACA), was signed as an executive order by Obama.

DACA allowed people who had arrived in the United States as children, often brought by their parents, to have deferred action from deportation for two years. They were also permitted to work legally

DACA RULES

Applicants to the DACA program had to follow strict guidelines to be accepted. They had to be at least 15 years old when they applied but younger than 31 as of June 15, 2012. They had to be younger than 16 when they entered the United States, living in the country continuously since June 15, 2007, and present in the country at the time they applied. DACA applicants had to be in high school, have graduated from high school, or have been honorably discharged from the military. Finally, to apply or remain in the program, individuals could not have committed a felony, a significant misdemeanor, or three or more minor misdemeanors.

in the country if they did not have felonies or serious misdemeanors on their record. The deferred action was renewable every two years.

DACA was implemented after the 2001 Development, Relief, and Education for Alien Minors (DREAM) Act—which would have provided these young people with a path to permanent residency—stalled in Congress. Approximately 800,000 people, called Dreamers, signed up for DACA.[11] Many of them were very young when they came to the United States and didn't even remember life in their countries of birth.

THE SLOWDOWN

The high number of people being arrested on suspicion of illegal immigration created a massive overload of the detention system. Dealing with this took a large amount of time and effort by ICE. The Obama administration decided this was detrimental to the original ICE mission.

In July 2015, a new policy replaced the Secure Communities initiative with the Priority Enforcement Program. The government would no longer target people trying to enter the United States near the border, noncriminal undocumented immigrants, or those who had overstayed visas.

Opponents of the Priority Enforcement Program believed the program made communities less safe. They felt that any infraction of immigration law should be enforced. But others argued that this returned ICE to its original mission, as stated by the Justice Department in 2004, to "prevent acts of terrorism by targeting the people, money, and materials that support terrorist and criminal activities."[12] In a five-day Operation Cross Check in 2015, ICE officers arrested 2,059 convicted criminals from 94 countries.[13] But the number of deportations in 2015 and 2016 were the lowest they had been in a decade.

> "THE ONLY PRIORITY CONTAINED IN THE PRIORITY ENFORCEMENT PROGRAM IS TO ENSURE THAT OUR IMMIGRATION LAWS ARE NOT ENFORCED IN THE INTERIOR OF THE UNITED STATES."[14]
>
> **—REPUBLICAN REPRESENTATIVE BOB GOODLATTE OF VIRGINIA**

FROM THE HEADLINES

FLIGHT FROM THE NORTHERN TRIANGLE

Since 2011, large numbers of child migrants have been crossing the US–Mexico border. In 2014, the number of unaccompanied children, many from Guatemala, El Salvador, and Honduras, was up 92 percent from the previous year.[15] This high number of children has overwhelmed the system to the point where they have been put in temporary detention centers. The Northern Triangle countries have seen increasing violence from gangs, drug cartels, and other organized crime since the late 2000s. Gangs target children as recruits. If children resist, the punishment by gang members could be rape, kidnapping, or murder. Under the Obama administration, DHS implemented measures to discourage immigration from the Northern Triangle. These measures included increased detention of women and children while they waited for asylum hearings and putting out information on the dangers of migrating. Between October 2015 and January 2016, apprehensions of families and unaccompanied children doubled compared with the same period the previous year. In January 2016, ICE conducted raids to find people who had been denied asylum. According to Secretary of Homeland Security Jeh Johnson, the focus of the raids was on families who had crossed the border illegally after May 1, 2014, and who had not obeyed orders to leave the country.

UNITED STATES

MEXICO

HONDURAS

GUATEMALA

EL SALVADOR

 NORTHERN TRIANGLE
COUNTRIES

CHAPTER SIX

ICE
CRACKDOWN

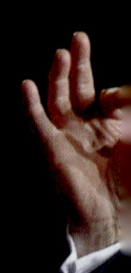

After President Trump took office in January 2017, the policies regarding ICE changed dramatically. During his presidential campaign, Trump had promised to deport every undocumented immigrant from the United States. To keep this promise, Trump signed an executive order in January 2017 that announced a policy to "ensure the faithful execution of the immigration laws of the United States . . . against all removable aliens."[1] He also ordered an increase of ICE staffing by 10,000 employees.[2] In April 2018, Attorney General Jeff Sessions announced a Zero Tolerance Policy. Under Obama, 21 percent of adults arrested for illegally crossing the border had been referred for

Stricter immigration policies were a key part of Trump's campaign, and once in office he took steps to put those policies into action.

prosecution.[3] The new policy mandated that all illegal border crossers be prosecuted.

Young people who had signed up for the DACA program worried that Trump would erase their right to stay in the United States. Still, approximately 8,000 new applications were filed each week as people sought protection from the crackdown. In total, an additional 200,000 people tried to enter the program.[4]

DEPORT THEM ALL?

Researchers have concluded that deporting every unauthorized person from the United States is not a practical solution to the immigration problem. The American Action Forum, a politically conservative think tank, estimated it would take 20 years to find and deport that many people at an estimated cost of $10,070 per person.[7] In addition, the economy would suffer due to the lack of labor, and society would be greatly impacted as families were broken apart. A 2013 Pew Research Center study showed that the median time an undocumented immigrant spent in the United States was 13 years. These people were closely integrated into their communities and the families of US citizens.

In September 2017, Trump announced the end of DACA. No new applications would be accepted. The two-year renewals for the approximately 800,000 people in the program would be processed until March 5, 2018.[5] After that time, an average of 915 DACA agreements would expire per day until the program ended in March 2020.[6] Without DACA protection, Dreamers became subject to deportation. Guidelines published by the US Citizenship and Immigration Services prioritized deportation for those who did not strictly follow immigration or criminal laws.

MORE DETAINEES

With the new policies, ICE detention facilities had to take care of increasing numbers of people. In 2016, ICE facilities held an average of 34,376 people per day.[8] By 2017, that number had increased to 39,322. ICE statistics showed that 51 percent of detainees were noncriminals who posed no threat to the community and that another 23 percent were people at the lowest threat level, typically meaning they had nonviolent convictions. Only 15 percent were classified as the highest threat level.[9]

> "I'M JUST A HUMAN BEING WHO CAME TO THIS COUNTRY LOOKING FOR BETTER OPPORTUNITIES. I HAVEN'T DONE ANYTHING WRONG. I BELONG IN THIS COUNTRY. THIS IS THE PLACE THAT I GREW UP IN AND WHERE MY FRIENDS AND FAMILY ARE."[11]
>
> —CAROLINA FUNG FENG, DACA RECIPIENT WHO IMMIGRATED FROM COSTA RICA AT AGE 12

As of November 2017, ICE oversaw 1,478 adult detention centers. Most of these, 71 percent, were operated by private prisons.[10] There were reports of inadequate health care, overcrowding, abuse, and unhygienic conditions. There were also complaints about high-risk detainees being housed with low-risk detainees.

All facilities were supposed to pass ICE inspections, but the DHS Office of Inspector General reported to Congress that the inspection system was inadequate. Contractors hired to do inspections did not have strict guidelines on what to report. Even when infractions were found by ICE inspectors, there was little follow-up, and few penalties were imposed. Inspectors frequently issued waivers for problems they found. Eight people died in ICE custody in 2019.

Like the US prison system, in 2020, ICE reported increasing numbers of detainees with COVID-19, a contagious disease that was spreading around the world with no cure. While many people could try to protect

THE DETENTION FACILITY NEXT DOOR

As ICE struggled to supply enough beds for all of its detainees, the agency resorted to leasing or buying various types of facilities to handle the overflow. One was in the basement of the building that housed Senator Ted Cruz's office in Austin, Texas. One was in Brooklyn, New York City, next to an Ikea store. Others are in hotels owned by major chains, at times in rooms guarded by ICE officers across the hall from hotel guests. Because these sites are considered temporary holding facilities, they are not on detainee tracking websites and are exempt from standards used by regular facilities. ICE has noted that these temporary holding sites are at times used for families, a better option than crowded holding cells in detention centers.

ICE detainees walk around Eloy Detention Center in Arizona.

themselves from the disease by wearing face masks, staying clean, and staying away from others, ICE detainees typically did not have that option in crowded detention centers. At least two ICE detainees had died from COVID-19 by June 2020, and thousands more were infected. In addition, the disease spread as immigrants were released into surrounding communities and deportees carried the virus to their home countries.

ICE UNDER PRESSURE

Although Trump's executive order had mandated 10,000 more ICE agents, the Office of Inspector General reported that ICE could not justify a need for this many more agents due to a lack of record keeping about its operations.

So, the increasing number of detainees housed by ICE put the agency's employees under more pressure.

On November 13, 2017, Chris Crane, head of the National ICE Council, which represents ICE employees, wrote a letter to Trump outlining grievances of the employees. In particular, he criticized the officials running the agency for corruption and lack of transparency. The letter also alleged that managers put field officers at risk by asking them "not to wear a bulletproof vest because illegal aliens might find it offensive."[12] Crane also said managers failed to support officers.

In addition, Crane accused managers of using cars and gas meant for officers in the field to commute to work. He accused managers of penalizing officers for taking earned vacation days

A COVER-UP?

In November 2017, ICE officers alleged that their managers tried to cover up an incident in which an undocumented man had been left shackled in a van for 37 hours without food or water. Hungry, dehydrated, and lying in his own waste, by the time he was discovered, he needed medical care. Instead, the man was dropped off a few hours later at a parking lot with minimal care. In addition, ICE officers alleged managers had dismissed immigration charges and told the man he could stay in the United States legally by applying for a visa—although this was not true— to discourage him from reporting the mistreatment. Although officers reported the incident to the director of ICE, Thomas Homan, they said the investigation was buried.

and sick leave. As Crane expressed on the National ICE Council website:

> As employees, military veterans, and law enforcement officers, we are ashamed of the problems that plague these federal agencies; we are ashamed of ICE leadership. We are ashamed of a Congress that just looks the other way and appears complicit. It's time for transparency, it's time to drain the swamp as the president committed to do.[13]

THE NEW PROPOSAL

On January 25, 2018, Trump presented a new four-point plan for immigration reform to Congress. Trump wanted to limit family sponsorships to spouses and minor children to end what is called chain migration, or large numbers of immigrants arriving when people come to the United States to live with family members already in the country. He also wanted to end the Diversity Immigrant Visa Program, often called the Visa Lottery. This program allows a limited number of people from countries with few migrants to the United States to apply for permanent residency.

Trump's plan proposed $25 billion in funding to build a wall between Mexico and the United States, as well as funding for more DHS employees, ICE attorneys, and immigration judges. He proposed ending all catch and release, instead wanting ICE to promptly remove people illegally crossing the border. He sought to detain and remove criminals in the country illegally and anyone overstaying a visa. He also proposed immigration court reforms to improve efficiency of the courts.

On January 9, 2018, a federal judge in the US District Court in San Francisco, California, blocked the government from discontinuing DACA renewals while lawsuits against the action were settled. With mounting pressure from the public to protect the young people who were part of DACA, Trump proposed a pathway to citizenship for DACA immigrants which would take ten to 12 years. The plan included all 1.8 million immigrants who were eligible for the DACA program.[14] This help for DACA recipients was tied to the other changes Trump proposed, such as the border wall.

Crane sent a letter to Trump in February 2018 outlining his objections to the plan. He said the president's proposal did nothing to help ICE in its efforts to enforce immigration laws. The proposal did not mention enforcing laws

Supporters of the DACA program held frequent protests in its defense.

against businesses that knowingly hired undocumented workers. Trump promised that these enforcement issues would come later, but in the end, Congress did not pass Trump's proposal, declaring that DACA recipients should not be held hostage to other immigration issues. By June 2018, ICE started moving up to 1,600 people awaiting deportation hearings out of the overcrowded detention centers and into federal prisons.[15] The Dreamers received a reprieve in June 2020 when the US Supreme Court declared that the Trump administration's efforts to end DACA were not legal because the administration did not provide adequate reasoning behind these efforts.

FROM THE
HEADLINES

THE WALL

One of Trump's campaign promises was to build a wall that stretched 2,000 miles (3,219 km) along the US–Mexico border to prevent illegal immigration into the United States. Proponents of the wall said it would reduce the number of undocumented immigrants and the smuggling of illegal items, especially drugs, that came into the United States. Opponents argued that the cost of the wall, with estimates ranging between $15 billion and $33 billion, far exceeded the benefits and that the vast stretches of desert along the border could be better monitored with less costly drones and other technology. Plus, they noted, in 2018 the majority of drugs crossing the southern border came through ports of entry. A wall would do nothing to prevent this. Environmentalists also opposed the

Trump toured a completed portion of the border wall in June 2020.

wall because it created a barrier to animals that migrated through the desert habitat along the border.

Congress did not authorize most of the money Trump wanted to fully build the wall, providing only $1.4 billion.[16] In 2019, the president declared a national emergency so he could move funds from other areas, such as money for building or updating military facilities, to build the wall. As of December 2019, 93 new miles (150 km) of wall had been built. Ninety miles (145 km) of that replaced existing walls and fences.

CHAPTER SEVEN

THE BREAKING POINT

Despite Trump's strict new policies, the number of people crossing the border illegally remained about the same as it was before. Adults picked up near the border were usually detained at a CBP facility. Those trying to get asylum were transferred to an ICE detention center. However, families were generally released while they awaited hearings in immigration court.

Then in early 2018, Trump instituted a policy that families would not be released while they awaited court hearings. Since US law prohibited children from being kept in adult facilities and there were not enough family detention centers, some children were separated from their parents so the parents could be

The Trump administration's policy that resulted in the separation of immigrant children from their families drew widespread condemnation.

detained. The parents went to adult detention centers, and the children were turned over to the US Department of Health and Human Services (HHS), which is tasked with caring for unaccompanied immigrant children. According to DHS, 2,342 children were separated from their parents between May 5 and June 9, 2018. HHS facilities reached 95 percent capacity.[1]

Images of children being taken from the arms of their parents and crying alone in fenced enclosures, as well as reports of the poor conditions in the child facilities, outraged many people. ICE, tasked with detaining and deporting undocumented immigrants, became a focal point for the wrath of opponents to Trump's new policy. As a result of an ACLU lawsuit, on June 26, 2018, US District Court Judge Dana Makoto Sabraw ordered that the children be returned to their parents. Children younger than five were to be returned within 14 days and older children within 30 days. However, the government

> "THE PRACTICE OF SEPARATING THESE FAMILIES WAS IMPLEMENTED WITHOUT ANY EFFECTIVE SYSTEM OR PROCEDURE. . . . THIS IS A STARTLING REALITY."[2]
>
> **—JUDGE SABRAW IN HIS ORDER TO REUNITE IMMIGRANT FAMILIES SEPARATED AT THE BORDER**

struggled to reunite families that quickly.

MORE PRESSURE

As of January 31, 2019, ICE had funds for detaining 40,500 people. The agency was actually detaining approximately 48,000 people.[3] Conditions at the detention centers were deteriorating. Reports from unannounced visits to ICE detention facilities in June found they were serving detainees expired food and offering no recreational activities. There were safety issues and moldy bathrooms. Politically liberal members of Congress wanted to cap the number of detention beds for undocumented immigrants at 16,500 to force the Trump administration to release detainees accused of misdemeanors or overstaying visas. Conservative members of Congress wanted to increase the number of beds to 52,000.[4]

REUNITING FAMILIES

After the government lost a lawsuit filed by the ACLU on behalf of children separated from their parents, government agencies began attempting to reunite children with parents. It was a monumental task. There were inadequate tracking records for the children who had been moved to facilities across the country. Some parents had already been deported, at times after being given the choice of taking their children back into dangerous countries or leaving them behind. On the day that 102 children under the age of five were to be reunited with their families, only 54 had been identified, located, and had their parents located.[5]

Meanwhile, ICE and the Border Patrol officers were processing hundreds of thousands of people arriving at the southern border or illegally crossing it. In March 2019, Crane sent another letter to Trump stating that the policies on the southern border were wasting resources. He said the policies prevented ICE agents from doing their primary job—catching undocumented criminals in the country.

Critics argued that some of the ICE resources spent along the southern border would be better spent on the agency's other missions.

In September 2019, DHS announced it would fully implement the end of the catch and release program that Trump had mandated shortly after taking office. This would include families entering the United States at the border. Acting Secretary of Homeland Security Kevin McAleenan said the end of catch and release was a reaction, in part, to the record number of 144,000 migrants apprehended or encountered at the southern border in May 2018, 72 percent of whom were families or unaccompanied children.[6]

A statement from DHS said, "If migrant family units do not claim fear of return, they will be quickly returned to their country of origin, in close collaboration with Central American countries. If they do claim fear, they will generally be returned to Mexico under the Migrant Protection Protocols."[7] The new Migrant Protection Protocols forced families seeking asylum to remain in Mexico while they waited for court dates in the United States. Opponents to this policy said that this put refugees in danger.

To keep migrants from traveling to the US border, the US government also began working with Mexico and the Northern Triangle countries to keep migrants in their home countries. In 2019, ICE agents worked in Guatemala with Guatemalan police to keep 300 migrants from Honduras from crossing into Guatemala.[8] The Trump administration also created agreements with the Northern Triangle countries that required immigrants to seek asylum in countries they crossed during their trip north. If they did not seek asylum in the other country, they would be deported back to that country once they reached the United States.

EXPEDITED REMOVAL

Trump also issued an executive order in 2017 to expand the program of expedited removal. DHS began drafting new orders which would expand expedited removal to people who had been in the United States less than two years rather than less than two weeks. The new order would also apply to people anywhere in the country instead of within 100 miles (161 km) of the border. DHS implemented the new orders in July 2019.

This gave ICE agents almost unchecked authority to deport undocumented immigrants they encountered for

ICE operates airplane flights to deport people to their countries of origin.

any reason. An apprehended person subject to removal had to prove to the ICE officer that they had been in the

JOE ARPAIO

The use of local authorities to enforce immigration has caused controversy in many communities across the United States. In 2009, a grand jury began investigating Joe Arpaio, the county sheriff of Arizona's Maricopa County, for civil rights violations. Maricopa County is the largest county in Arizona, with a population of 4.4 million.[10] It includes the state's capital, Phoenix. Approximately one-third of the population is Hispanic. Complaints included immigration patrols that did sweeps of Hispanic people gathered near businesses. Hispanic people were four to nine times more likely to be stopped in traffic stops, and 20 percent of the stops were done without a plausible reason. Hispanic people in jails were punished with up to 23 hours a day of solitary confinement for not understanding English instructions. In 2011, US District Judge G. Murray Snow issued an injunction barring Arpaio from detaining people based only on their immigration status. Arpaio defied the order. In July 2017, the sheriff was found guilty of criminal contempt for ignoring the order to stop racial profiling by local authorities. President Trump pardoned him in August 2017.

United States for more than two years or that they were legally in the country. The decision to deport an individual was up to the ICE officer, and people were detained until deportation with no right to appeal. In 2017, 35 percent of all deportations were done through expedited removal. This number was expected to drastically increase under the new 2019 guidelines.[9] However, in September 2019, the federal district court for the District of Columbia issued an injunction that prevented expanding expedited removal.

New rules also pulled USCIS into enforcement. In a new policy, immigrants could be put into deportation proceedings if they applied for a modification of a visa, green card, or naturalization paper and were denied. They could also be subject to possible deportation if they were charged with a crime or had been involved in any activity that DHS considered a crime regardless of whether they had been arrested or charged. In addition, ICE officers could detain anyone they found not obeying a notice to appear in court for deportation proceedings.

CHAPTER EIGHT

RESISTANCE

P eople began questioning the policies and effectiveness of ICE, especially after the child-separation cases in 2018. ICE's budget had grown from $3.3 billion in 2003 to more than $7 billion in 2018.[1] Its budget request for 2019 was $8.8 billion, including money for 2,000 new ICE agents and an increase in detention beds.[2] Critics charged that ICE's focus had shifted from keeping the United States safe from criminals and terrorists to detaining and deporting people crossing the border.

ICE was accused of abusive practices and of targeting people who had no criminal behavior other than crossing the border illegally. Many people saw ICE as terrorizing undocumented immigrants, their families, and their communities. Rumors of ICE raids closed

ICE's 2019 budget request included funding for large increases in the agency's staff and facilities.

down communities as people stayed home from work and school to avoid the raids.

In addition to detaining undocumented immigrants and handling deportations, ICE agents still continued to target smugglers, human traffickers, and other criminal enterprises. However, public attention was on ICE's overcrowded detention facilities and what was considered a humanitarian crisis at the border. CBP was responsible for detaining immigrants on the border, but most people agreed there was a need for at least some level of border protection. ICE is responsible for transportation and detention of the people arrested by CBP. So, prominent critics of US immigration policies, including members of Congress, focused on ICE, questioning whether the agency was out of control.

PROBLEMS WITH ICE PARTNERSHIPS

Since the implementation of 287(g), which allowed ICE to officially work with state and local law enforcement, there were legal objections to the policy. One objection was that the policy did not target the high-level criminals that ICE was supposed to target. The Migration Policy Institute, an organization that examines international migration issues, found that half of all the detainer requests issued under the program were for people with misdemeanors or traffic offenses. In some states, especially in the Southeast, detainers were used by local officials to target undocumented immigrants rather than for arresting criminals. In other investigations, local officials used the system for racial profiling by conducting sweeps of Hispanic neighborhoods or setting up roadblocks at the entrances to these neighborhoods.

ICE has partnerships with other law enforcement agencies, including local police departments.

Another point of contention with the 287(g) partnerships was the cost to the communities. ICE paid for training, but local governments had to pay for travel, lodging, and food while their officers trained. Local governments also paid salaries, including overtime, to officers and paid for supplies. Local governments paid most of the costs for detaining suspects until they could be turned over to ICE.

In addition to 287(g), other ICE programs worked with jails in local communities. The Criminal Alien Program allowed ICE to screen federal and state prisons and local jails daily to identify undocumented immigrants for deportation. The Secure Communities program ran the fingerprints of anyone arrested through an immigration database. Those identified could be detained until ICE arrived to take custody.

Finally, communities found that using local officers to enforce federal immigration laws led many immigrants to not trust their local police. This made enforcing laws and arresting criminals more difficult for local officers. People were unwilling to cooperate with police for fear of deportation of themselves, family members, or friends.

SANCTUARY CITIES

Federal law does not require local governments to help ICE enforce immigration laws. Sanctuary cities, or sanctuary counties or states, are communities that have policies or laws that limit cooperation between ICE and local law enforcement. Some enforcement agencies may refuse to sign cooperation agreements with ICE. Others may refuse to detain people in jail beyond their release date while they wait for ICE to pick them up. Still others may refuse to turn people over to ICE without an official warrant.

In January 2017, Trump signed an executive order that

THE HISTORY OF SANCTUARY CITIES

Early predecessors to sanctuary cities arose in the 1790s to protect Black people who had escaped from enslavement. These fugitive slaves were primarily fleeing from Southern states to Northern states. The Fugitive Slave Act of 1793 authorized state and local authorities to seize and return fugitive slaves. However, some states tried to pass laws that protected the rights of enslaved people. In 1842, the US Supreme Court decided in the case of *Prigg v. Pennsylvania* that returning slaves to the white people who had enslaved them was a federal matter. States could not pass laws concerning either protection of or return of enslaved people. On the other hand, federal officials could not force state officers to enforce federal laws. This idea of a division between the powers of the federal government and state governments is seen again today in terms of undocumented immigrants. The modern idea of sanctuary cities for immigrants began in the 1980s. The first sanctuaries were churches that provided sanctuary from federal authorities to Northern Triangle refugees. In 1985, San Francisco became the first sanctuary city by passing laws that forbade police from assisting federal immigration officers.

allowed the federal government to withhold grant money from sanctuary cities for not cooperating with ICE. In April, Judge William H. Orrick of the US District Court temporarily blocked the order, ruling that Trump did not have authority to withhold funding to make communities cooperate with immigration enforcement. Three federal courts upheld the ruling. However, the Second US Circuit Court of Appeals ruled in February 2020 that money granted by the federal government to local law enforcement could be withheld. In early 2020, there were 11 sanctuary states, approximately 130 sanctuary counties, and 37 sanctuary cities.[3]

Some states have gone in the opposite direction, passing laws forcing local law enforcement to cooperate with ICE. In 2017, Texas passed a law that allows local police to ask about a person's immigration status. The law also states that local governments cannot forbid their police from contacting ICE. Other states have outright banned sanctuary cities.

"OUR OFFICERS WILL NOT HAVE THEIR HANDS TIED BY SANCTUARY RULES WHEN ENFORCING IMMIGRATION LAWS TO REMOVE CRIMINAL ALIENS FROM OUR COMMUNITIES."[4]

—DAVID JENNINGS, ICE FIELD OFFICE DIRECTOR IN SAN FRANCISCO, CALIFORNIA

In 2019, ICE had 77 agreements with law enforcement agencies across the country. The patchwork of local laws gave ICE officers in the field hundreds of different ways to interact with local authorities. Meanwhile, some states were passing new laws to reduce the authority of ICE within their states. California passed a law requiring ICE officers to have a warrant to make an immigration arrest inside a courthouse. When ICE officers arrested a man without a warrant at the courthouse anyway, local authorities were angry. However, federal immigration officials claim they are not bound by state laws. It is uncertain whether local officials can enforce laws to prevent ICE arrests at courthouses.

MORE TO THE
STORY

SANCTUARY CITIES AND THE CONSTITUTION

Many people do not realize that undocumented immigrants have rights under the US Constitution. The Fourth Amendment guarantees freedom from unreasonable search and seizure. This means that law enforcement must have probable cause, and usually a search warrant, to search people or enter their homes. Several courts have ruled that detaining people without cause is a violation of the Fourth Amendment. The 14th Amendment states that all citizens and any people living within US jurisdiction have equal protection under the law. In the 1896 case *Wong Wing v. United States*, the Supreme Court reinforced this, stating, "These provisions are universal in their application to all persons."[5] Supporters of sanctuary cities have also called them Constitutional cities because once people suspected of being in the country illegally have been cleared of criminal charges, have been released on bail, or have completed jail time, police in a sanctuary city will release them. In a non-sanctuary city, the state or local enforcement agencies may continue to hold people until ICE can arrest them. Sanctuary cities still cooperate with ICE to turn over dangerous criminals to the federal authorities.

THE MOVEMENT TO ABOLISH ICE

By 2018, some people began to believe that the concerns surrounding ICE were too much to fix. They called for abolishing the agency. In June 2018, Democratic representative Mark Pocan of Wisconsin said he would introduce legislation to eliminate the agency in favor of an immigration enforcement system that "upholds the dignity of all individuals."[6] His proposal envisioned creating a commission to examine the duties of ICE that need to be maintained, such as catching terrorists, and ones that should be taken away because they have been abused or do not fit the agency's mission.

"ICE is not working in its current form because the president has abused it to go after people with parking tickets, traffic violations, etc., rather than focusing on domestic terrorism and human trafficking and the big crimes," Pocan said.[7]

> "ICE REPRESENTS THE IDEA THAT ALL IMMIGRATION IS DANGEROUS AND A THREAT TO OUR SECURITY."[8]
>
> —HEMANTH GUNDAVARAM OF THE IMMIGRANT JUSTICE CLINIC AT NORTHEASTERN UNIVERSITY

Other members of Congress agree. Democratic representative Alexandria Ocasio-Cortez has become a leading proponent for abolishing ICE. She came to national attention when she defeated a longtime New York Democratic representative, Joe Crowley, with a much more politically liberal platform that included shutting down ICE. "It's time to abolish ICE, clear the path to citizenship, and protect the rights of families to remain together," Ocasio-Cortez said.[9] Democratic senator Kirsten Gillibrand agreed, saying, "I believe you should get rid of

Representative Alexandria Ocasio-Cortez speaks at a 2019 rally calling on the government to cut funding for ICE.

[ICE], start over, reimagine it, and build something that actually works."[10]

Some proponents of keeping ICE argued that abolishing the agency would mean open borders where anyone could enter. President Trump strongly opposed abolishing ICE, saying in a tweet, "Every day, the brave men and women of ICE are liberating communities from savage gangs like MS-13. We will NOT stand for these vile Democrat smears in law enforcement. We will always stand proudly with the BRAVE HEROES of ICE and BORDER PATROL!"[11] Republican senators Jim Inhofe of Oklahoma and John Kennedy of Louisiana introduced a resolution in support of ICE, cosponsored by a dozen other Republican senators. Republican senator Chuck Grassley of Iowa wrote, "Calls to abolish ICE are misguided and dangerous."[12]

Although the move to completely abolish ICE has not gained popular support, many people in Congress do believe that the agency needs a thorough reexamination. Democratic senator Chuck Schumer of New York has said that ICE needs reform but does not believe it should be abolished.

CHAPTER NINE

WHAT HAPPENS NEXT?

Despite the attempts to deport large numbers of undocumented immigrants and prevent those seeking asylum from entering the country, the US undocumented-immigrant population remains in the millions. Approximately one-fourth of all immigrants are undocumented.[1] Most of these immigrants live in cities and make up a significant part of the population. Officials estimate that in Texas, about 8.7 percent of people in the Houston area and 6.9 percent in the Dallas area are undocumented immigrants.[2]

The ICE Enforcement and Removal Operations Report for 2019 reported 1.15 million people were apprehended nationwide, a 68 percent increase over 2018. CBP agents apprehended 851,508 people, a

An ICE officer stands outside a chartered deportation flight from Texas to India.

COUNTING UNDOCUMENTED IMMIGRANTS

The US Census Bureau, which is responsible for counting the number of people in the United States, surveys about two million households every year. It asks whether anyone in a household is foreign-born. This may include people who are naturalized citizens, permanent residents (green card holders), refugees, or undocumented people. They then subtract the people whom DHS identifies as naturalized citizens or permanent residents and the people whom DHS identifies as refugees. The rest are assumed to be undocumented immigrants. The government knows that many people will not be counted since they won't answer the survey. DHS estimates this number to be approximately 10 percent, so it adjusts the number counted accordingly. No one knows how accurate this number is. The number of undocumented immigrants may be much lower or much greater than the official estimates.

115 percent increase over 2018.[3] More than half of those were members of apprehended families, the highest number on record.

The high numbers of arrests have continued to keep ICE very busy. According to the report, these numbers demonstrate "both the magnitude and the changing demographics that have fueled a border security and humanitarian crisis and have compromised ICE's ability to conduct enforcement."[4]

The 2019 report also noted that ICE's Fugitive Operations resources have not increased for many years, although the makeup of unauthorized migration has shifted since 2010 to include more visa overstays than border crossings. In 2016, the Center for Migration Studies estimated that 62 percent of undocumented immigrants had overstayed visas as opposed to 38 percent who had come across the border illegally.[5]

POSSIBLE SOLUTIONS

ICE enforces immigration laws passed by Congress. Its work is guided by the priorities set by the presidential administration in power. While previous administrations had enforced policies concentrating on security, terrorism, and removing criminals, Trump's policies resulted in more efforts to reduce all unauthorized immigration to the United States and to remove all undocumented immigrants from the country.

Some members of ICE worried that a focus on immigration enforcement took resources away from other ICE priorities, such as policing cybercrimes.

In June 2018, a group of 19 ICE investigation agents asked Secretary of Homeland Security Kirstjen Nielsen to break apart different functions of ICE. Agents in Homeland Security Investigations (HSI) felt that dealing with detention and deportation meant they did not have the resources to deal with the original mandate of the agency—national security, organized crime, smuggling, and human trafficking. The shift in immigration policy had resulted in funding being shifted from HSI to other areas of ICE for immigration enforcement outside of the criminal court system.

The agents suggested restructuring ICE into two subagencies: HSI and Enforcement and Removal Operations (ERO). HSI would handle the ICE mission of investigating transnational

RETURN OF LETTER

ICE continues to catch smugglers. In June 2018, ICE and the Department of Justice returned a 500-year-old copy of a letter from Christopher Columbus to Spain. The letter, manually copied in 1493 from a letter written by Columbus, described Columbus's discoveries in the Americas. The letter was stolen from the National Library of Catalonia in Barcelona, Spain. The ICE investigation that resulted in the return of the letter took seven years. Following a tip, ICE investigators discovered that the letter in the National Library was a forgery; the original had been stolen. They identified the original, which had been sold in June 2011. By investigating smugglers, ICE has returned more than 11,000 stolen artifacts to other countries, including paintings, manuscripts, dinosaur fossils, cultural artifacts, and even a mummy's hand.[6]

border security involving cybercrime, smuggling, and human trafficking. ERO would concentrate its attention on detaining and removing undocumented immigrants from the country.

REDUCING NUMBERS

To address the problems facing ICE and CBP, Democratic members of the House of Representatives proposed new priorities for detention and deportation. This might mean releasing immigrants awaiting court dates as had been done in the past. Another alternative to detention is the Intensive Supervision Appearance Program, which releases people under supervision using such tools as house arrest–monitoring ankle bracelets. This costs the government $4.04 per day. Detention, on the other hand, costs $130 per day for an adult and at least $320 per day for a child.[7]

The number of people on existing alternative programs increased from 23,000 in 2014 to 96,000 in 2019. However, 2019 data indicates that these alternative programs often are not effective. Approximately one-fourth of family members in 2019 disappeared before their court dates.[8] ICE does not have the funding or staffing to monitor or locate these people.

Some Democratic politicians have suggested decriminalizing border crossings. Under federal law, anyone who crosses the border illegally can be charged in criminal court with a misdemeanor and punished by up to six months in prison. In the past this law was often ignored, but the number of prosecutions has gradually increased beginning with the Bush and Obama administrations.

Although government studies show that increased prosecution was not an effective way to deter border crossers, under the Trump administration the number of these prosecutions went up 40 percent, clogging the detention centers and court system.[9] Proponents of decriminalizing border crossings say criminal prosecution is unnecessary because crossing the border illegally, just like overstaying a visa, is also a civil offense that can be judged in immigration court and punished by deportation. Opponents to this proposition believe that making illegal border crossing only a civil offense, and no longer a crime, is opening the border to more illegal crossings.

CHANGES?

As immigration has become an increasingly politicized issue in the United States, a lot of public attention has focused on ICE. Some people believe ICE's problems could be solved through restructuring the agency or reforming immigration policies. Others want to abolish ICE altogether, while others still believe the agency is operating fine the way it is.

Regardless of what members of the public or even what individual ICE agents themselves want, ICE's operations are in the hands of the federal government. Congress can pass laws addressing the status of the millions of undocumented immigrants in the country. It can change laws regarding who can enter the country legally. It has the power to fund immigration courts. As long as people continue immigrating to the United States without permission, and as long as ICE is tasked with enforcing immigration laws, the debate over how illegal immigration should be addressed is likely to continue.

"THE AMERICAN DREAM IS NOT A SPRINT, OR EVEN A MARATHON, BUT A RELAY. OUR FAMILIES DON'T ALWAYS CROSS THE FINISH LINE IN ONE GENERATION."[10]

—FORMER US SECRETARY OF HOUSING AND URBAN DEVELOPMENT JULIÁN CASTRO, A DEMOCRAT

ESSENTIAL
FACTS

MAJOR EVENTS

- US Immigration and Customs Enforcement (ICE) begins operations in 2003 as part of the newly formed Department of Homeland Security.

- In 2006, ICE expands working with local and state law enforcement under the 287(g) program.

- In 2015, President Barack Obama begins the Priority Enforcement Program to focus on catching undocumented immigrants who pose a danger to the United States. The number of people deported decreases.

- The Trump administration declares a Zero Tolerance Policy in 2018, which leads to ICE stopping and detaining large numbers of undocumented immigrants entering or living in the United States.

- Parent-child separations of immigrants at the US–Mexico border in 2018 result in calls to abolish ICE.

KEY PLAYERS

- President George W. Bush formed ICE with the Department of Homeland Security in 2002.

- President Obama created Deferred Action for Childhood Arrivals (DACA) in 2012 to protect unauthorized immigrants brought to the United States as children from deportation.

- President Donald Trump's 2016 campaign platform included calls to remove all undocumented immigrants from the nation and to better secure its borders.

IMPACT ON SOCIETY

ICE's mission is to fight international criminal activity that crosses the border, such as smuggling, human trafficking, and terrorism. ICE also enforces immigration laws. The agency has received criticism for deporting noncriminals and holding large numbers of undocumented immigrants in detention. This has stressed ICE's relationship with states and cities where undocumented immigrants are important parts of the community. Some people have called for abolishing ICE. Others have said the agency is doing its job, while still others argue ICE should be maintained but reformed.

QUOTE

"I'm just a human being who came to this country looking for better opportunities. I haven't done anything wrong. I belong in this country."

—*Carolina Fung Feng, DACA recipient*

GLOSSARY

ASYLUM
Protection given by a country to someone who has left his or her country as a political refugee.

BOND
A fee paid by someone else so that an accused person can be released from jail until the case has concluded.

DEPORT
To force someone to leave a country.

DETENTION
The act of holding a person in custody.

FUGITIVE
A person who runs away to avoid capture.

INDICT
To formally accuse someone of a crime.

INJUNCTION

A legal order that stops a person from starting or continuing an action that threatens another's legal rights.

PERMANENT RESIDENT

An immigrant who has a legal status to stay in a country although not a citizen.

PORT OF ENTRY

An airport, harbor, or land crossing on a border where customs officials allow authorized entry into the country.

PROSECUTION

Conducting legal proceedings against someone accused of a crime.

REFUGEE

Someone who has fled his or her country and cannot return to it for fear of harm or death.

SHELL COMPANY

A company used primarily to facilitate movement of money or tax evasion.

VISA

An official authorization permitting entry into and travel within a country.

WARRANT

A document allowing law enforcement to carry out an arrest, a search, or an information-gathering operation.

ADDITIONAL
RESOURCES

SELECTED BIBLIOGRAPHY

"Celebrating the History of ICE." *US ICE*, 1 Mar. 2019, ice.gov. Accessed 2 July 2020.

Hannah Dreier. "Trust and Consequences." *Washington Post*, 15 Feb. 2020, washingtonpost.com. Accessed 2 July 2020.

Sophia Yapalater. "A Tale of Two Immigrant Detainees." *American Civil Liberties Union*, 8 Dec. 2014, aclu.org. Accessed 2 July 2020.

FURTHER READINGS

Carser, A. R. *US Immigration Policy*. Abdo, 2018.

Cummings, Judy Dodge. *Immigration Nation: The American Identity in the Twenty-First Century*. Nomad, 2019.

Harris, Duchess, and Nina Judith Katz. *The Dreamers and DACA*. Abdo, 2019.

ONLINE RESOURCES

To learn more about US Immigration and Customs Enforcement, please visit **abdobooklinks.com** or scan this QR code. These links are routinely monitored and updated to provide the most current information available.

MORE INFORMATION

For more information on this subject, contact or visit the following organizations:

American Civil Liberties Union

125 Broad St., Eighteenth Floor
New York, NY 10004
212-549-2500
aclu.org
The ACLU is a nonprofit organization that provides legal aid in many types of civil rights cases, including immigration cases.

Border Patrol Museum & Gift Shop

4315 Woodrow Bean Transmountain Rd.
El Paso, TX 79924
915-759-6060
borderpatrolmuseum.com
This museum provides a history of the US Border Patrol and immigration enforcement, including exhibits on historical vehicles and uniforms.

SOURCE
NOTES

CHAPTER 1. THE ENFORCER

1. "Combating Gangs." *US ICE*, 13 Feb. 2020, ice.gov. Accessed 28 July 2020.
2. Michael S. Williamson. "Trust and Consequences." *Washington Post*, 15 Feb. 2020, washingtonpost.com. Accessed 28 July 2020.
3. Williamson, "Trust and Consequences."
4. "American Psychological Association Calls for Immediate Halt to Sharing Immigrant Youths' Confidential Psychotherapy Notes with ICE." *American Psychological Association*, 17 Feb. 2020, apa.org. Accessed 29 July 2020.
5. Jeffrey S. Passel. "Measuring Illegal Immigration: How Pew Research Center Counts Unauthorized Immigrants in the U.S." *Pew Research Center*, 12 July 2019, pewresearch.org. Accessed 28 July 2020.
6. "How the United States Immigration System Works." *American Immigration Council*, 10 Oct. 2019, americanimmigrationcouncil.org. Accessed 28 July 2020.
7. Jeffrey S. Passel and D'Vera Cohn. "Size of U.S. Unauthorized Immigrant Workforce Stable after the Great Recession." *Pew Research Center*, 3 Nov. 2016, pewresearch.org. Accessed 28 July 2020.

CHAPTER 2. THE ORIGIN OF ICE

1. "September 11 Attacks." *History.com*, 11 Sept. 2019, history.com. Accessed 28 July 2020.
2. Sarah E. Murphy. "Federal Immigration Agencies Overview." *Border Immigration Lawyer*, 2020, borderimmigrationlawyer.com. Accessed 28 July 2020.
3. "History." *US ICE*, 13 May 2020, ice.gov. Accessed 28 July 2020.
4. "Frequently Asked Questions (FAQs)." *US ICE*, 2 Apr. 2019, ice.gov. Accessed 28 July 2020.
5. "U.S. Immigration and Customs Enforcement." *AllGov*, 2016, allgov.com. Accessed 28 July 2020.
6. "Frequently Asked Questions (FAQs)."
7. "Episode 4: What's It Like to Be a Deportation Officer with ERO?" *US ICE*, n.d., ice.gov. Accessed 28 July 2020.
8. "Office of the Chief Immigration Judge." *United States Department of Justice*, 27 May 2020, justice.gov. Accessed 28 July 2020.
9. "Fact Sheet: Immigration Courts." *National Immigration Forum*, 7 Aug. 2018, immigrationforum.org. Accessed 28 July 2020.

CHAPTER 3. INTERNATIONAL EFFORTS

1. "ICE HSI, CBP Operation Seizes Record-Breaking $123 Million of Fake Sports Merchandise." *US ICE*, 30 Jan. 2020, ice.gov. Accessed 28 July 2020.
2. "ICE Seizes 181,000 Counterfeit Items Worth Nearly $43 Million in Laredo, Texas." *US ICE*, 16 Oct. 2018, ice.gov. Accessed 28 July 2020.
3. Nick Givas. "$123M In Fake Super Bowl Merch Seized by CBP, DHS, ICE Ahead of Big Game." *Fox News*, 1 Feb. 2020, foxnews.com. Accessed 28 July 2020.
4. Victoria A. Greenfield, Blas Nuñez-Neto, Ian Mitch, Joseph C. Chang, and Etienne Rosas. "Human Smuggling and Associated Revenues." *Homeland Security Operational Analysis Center*, 2019, rand.org. Accessed 28 July 2020.

5. John DeGarmo. "The Shocking Truth of Child Sex Trafficking." *HuffPost*, 18 Nov. 2016, huffpost.com. Accessed 28 July 2020.

6. "11 Facts about Human Trafficking." *DoSomething.org*, n.d., dosomething.org. Accessed 28 July 2020.

7. "Operation Predator – Targeting Child Exploitation and Sexual Crimes." *US ICE*, 25 June 2012, ice.gov. Accessed 28 July 2020.

8. "Operation Predator – Targeting Child Exploitation and Sexual Crimes."

9. "Human Trafficking." *US ICE*, 13 Feb. 2020, ice.gov. Accessed 28 July 2020.

10. "Cyber Crimes Center." *US ICE*, 11 Dec. 2019, ice.gov. Accessed 28 July 2020.

CHAPTER 4. IMMIGRATION ENFORCEMENT

1. "Celebrating the History of ICE." *US ICE*, 1 Mar. 2019, ice.gov. Accessed 28 July 2020.

2. "Celebrating the History of ICE."

3. "Celebrating the History of ICE."

4. Nick Miroff. "After an ICE Raid, Few Americans Showed Up to Work at This Texas Meatpacking Plant." *Texas Tribune*, 5 Mar. 2018, texastribune.org. Accessed 28 July 2020.

5. Miroff, "After an ICE Raid."

6. "ICE Delivers More than 5,200 I-9 Audit Notices to Businesses across the US in 2-Phase Nationwide Operation." *US ICE*, 24 July 2018, ice.gov. Accessed 28 July 2020.

7. Rogelio V. Solis and Jeff Amy. "ICE Raids at Chicken Plants Net 680 Arrests." *Times Union*, 7 Aug. 2019, timesunion.com. Accessed 28 July 2020.

8. Miroff, "After an ICE Raid."

CHAPTER 5. CHANGING PRIORITIES

1. Bethania Palma and David Mikkelson. "Were More People Deported under the Obama Administration than Any Other?" *Snopes*, 20 Oct. 2016, snopes.com. Accessed 28 July 2020.

2. Livia Luan. "Profiting from Enforcement: The Role of Private Prisons in U.S. Immigration Detention." *Migration Policy Institute*, 2 May 2018, migrationpolicy.org. Accessed 28 July 2020.

3. "ICE Arrests More than 3,100 Convicted Criminal Aliens and Immigration Fugitives in Nationwide Operation." *US ICE*, 2 Apr. 2012, ice.gov. Accessed 28 July 2020.

4. Clyde Haberman. "For Private Prisons, Detaining Immigrants Is Big Business." *New York Times*, 1 Oct. 2018, nytimes.com. Accessed 28 July 2020.

5. Monsy Alvarado et. al. "'These People Are Profitable': Under Trump, Private Prisons Are Cashing in on ICE Detainees." *USA Today*, 20 Dec. 2019, usatoday.com. Accessed 28 July 2020.

6. Heather Timmons. "No One Really Knows What ICE Is Supposed to Be. Politicians Love That." *Quartz*, 7 July 2018, qz.com. Accessed 28 July 2020.

7. "Celebrating the History of ICE." *US ICE*, 1 Mar. 2019, ice.gov. Accessed 28 July 2020.

8. "ICE Arrests More than 3,100."

9. "A Primer on Expedited Removal." *American Immigration Council*, 22 July 2019, americanimmigrationcouncil.org. Accessed 28 July 2020.

10. Dara Lind. "The 2014 Central American Migrant Crisis." *Vox*, 10 Oct. 2014, vox.com. Accessed 28 July 2020.

11. Katie Heinrich and Daniel Arkin. "What Is DACA? Here's What You Need to Know about the Program Trump Is Ending." *NBC News*, 5 Sept. 2017, nbcnews.com. Accessed 28 July 2020.

12. Brian A. Reaves. "Federal Law Enforcement Officers, 2004." *US Department of Justice*, July 2006, bjs.gov. Accessed 28 July 2020.

13. Palma and Mikkelson, "Were More People Deported under the Obama Administration?"

14. "Obama Administration Implements Priority Enforcement Program, Limits Interior Enforcement." *NumbersUSA*, 8 July 2015, numbersusa.com. Accessed 28 July 2020.

15. Amanda Taub. "The Awful Reason Tens of Thousands of Children Are Seeking Refuge in the United States." *Vox*, 30 June 2014, vox.com. Accessed 28 July 2020.

CHAPTER 6. ICE CRACKDOWN

1. "Executive Order: Enhancing Public Safety in the Interior of the United States." *White House*, 25 Jan. 2017, whitehouse.gov. Accessed 28 July 2020.

2. Jamiles Lartey. "US Immigration: What Is Ice and Why Is It Controversial?" *Guardian*, 4 July 2018, theguardian.com. Accessed 28 July 2020.

SOURCE NOTES CONTINUED

3. Lori Robertson. "Fact Check: Did the Obama Administration Separate Families?" *USA Today*, 23 June 2018, usatoday.com. Accessed 28 July 2020.

4. Lori Robertson. "The Facts on DACA." *FactCheck.org*, 22 Jan. 2018, factcheck.org. Accessed 28 July 2020.

5. Katie Heinrich and Daniel Arkin. "What Is DACA? Here's What You Need to Know about the Program Trump Is Ending." *NBC News*, 5 Sept. 2017, nbcnews.com. Accessed 28 July 2020.

6. Robertson, "The Facts on DACA."

7. "Donald Trump Wants to Deport Every Single Illegal Immigrant—Could He?" *BBC*, 11 Nov. 2015, bbc.com. Accessed 28 July 2020.

8. "Congressional Hearings Show 50% Growth in ICE Detention under Trump Despite Dysfunctional and Incompetent Inspections System that Fails to Keep People Safe." *America's Voice*, 27 Sept. 2019, americasvoice.org. Accessed 28 July 2020.

9. Leanna Garfield, Shayanne Gal, and Andy Kiersz. "Migrant Detention Centers in the US Are Under Fire for Their 'Horrifying' Conditions—and There's at Least One in Every State. This Map Shows Which Have the Most." *Business Insider*, 5 July 2019, businessinsider.com. Accessed 28 July 2020.

10. Garfield, Gal, and Kiersz. "Migrant Detention Centers in the US Are Under Fire."

11. Camilo Montoya-Galvez. "Young Undocumented Immigrants Turn to Supreme Court to Save DACA." *CBS News*, 12 Nov. 2019, cbsnews.com. Accessed 28 July 2020.

12. Carlos Ballesteros. "President Trump Stabbed Supporters in the Back, ICE Union Head Says." *Newsweek*, 16 Nov. 2017, newsweek.com. Accessed 28 July 2020.

13. Bob Price. "Report: Trump to Meet with ICE Union over 'Grievances.'" *Breitbart*, 27 Nov. 2017, breitbart.com. Accessed 28 July 2020.

14. Stephen Dinan. "Exclusive: ICE Agents See 'Gaping Holes' in Trump's Immigration Plan." *Washington Times*, 4 Feb. 2018, washingtontimes.com. Accessed 28 July 2020.

15. Alan Gomez. "ICE to Send 1,600 Immigration Violators to Federal Prisons." *USA Today*, 8 June 2018, usatoday.com. Accessed 28 July 2020.

16. David Smith. "Trump Declares National Emergency to Build US-Mexico Border Wall." *Guardian*, 15 Feb. 2019, theguardian.com. Accessed 28 July 2020.

CHAPTER 7. THE BREAKING POINT

1. Lori Robertson. "Fact Check: Did the Obama Administration Separate Families?" *USA Today*, 23 June 2018, usatoday.com. Accessed 28 July 2020.

2. Laura Jarrett. "Federal Judge Orders Reunification of Parents and Children, End to Most Family Separations at Border." *CNN*, 27 June 2018, cnn.com. Accessed 28 July 2020.

3. Katie Shepherd. "Government Quietly Increases ICE Detention to 48,000 Beds During the Shutdown." *Immigration Impact*, 31 Jan. 2019, immigrationimpact.com. Accessed 28 July 2020.

4. Brian Naylor. "ICE Detention Beds New Stumbling Block in Efforts to Prevent Another Shutdown." *NPR*, 11 Feb. 2019, npr.org. Accessed 28 July 2020.

5. Kevin Liptak, Daniella Diaz, and Sophie Tatum. "Trump Pardons Former Sheriff Joe Arpaio." *CNN*, 27 Aug. 2017, cnn.com. Accessed 28 July 2020.

6. Richard Gonzales. "Trump Administration to End 'Catch and Release' Immigration Policy, Says DHS Chief." *NPR*, 24 Sept. 2019, npr.org. Accessed 28 July 2020.

7. Gonzales, "Trump Administration to End 'Catch and Release' Immigration Policy, Says DHS Chief."

8. Bob Price and Ildefonso Ortiz. "Hundreds of Caravan Migrants Deported to Honduras by Guatemalan Police, U.S. ICE Agents." *Breitbart*, 19 Jan. 2020, breitbart.com. Accessed 28 July 2020.

9. "Fact Sheet: Immigration Courts." *National Immigration Forum*, 7 Aug. 2018, immigrationforum.org. Accessed 28 July 2020.

10. "Maricopa County, Arizona Population 2020." *World Population Review*, 2020, worldpopulationreview.com. Accessed 28 July 2020.

CHAPTER 8. RESISTANCE

1. Julianne Hing. "What Does It Mean to Abolish ICE?" *Nation*, 11 July 2018, thenation.com. Accessed 28 July 2020.

2. "Stronger Border Security." *Executive Office of the President of the United States*, 2019, whitehouse.gov. Accessed 28 July 2020.

3. Bryan Griffith and Jessica M. Vaughan. "Map: Sanctuary Cities, Counties, and States." *Center for Immigration Studies*, 23 Mar. 2020, cis.org. Accessed 28 July 2020.

4. Arlene Martinez. "In California: ICE Ignores State Immigration Laws." *USA Today*, 20 Feb. 2020, usatoday.com. Accessed 28 July 2020.

5. Matthew Green. "What Legal Rights Do Undocumented Immigrants Have? (With Lesson Plan)." *KQED*, 28 Mar. 2017, kqed.org. Accessed 28 July 2020.

6. John Bacon. "ICE on Ice? Move to Abolish ICE, at Center of Storm in Immigration Battle, Has a Long Way To Go." *USA Today*, 28 June 2018, usatoday.com. Accessed 28 July 2020.

7. Sarah D. Wire. "Democrats' Push to Abolish ICE Reaches Capitol Hill." *Los Angeles Times*, 12 July 2018, latimes.com. Accessed 28 July 2020.

8. Bacon, "ICE on Ice?"

9. Wire, "Democrats' Push to Abolish ICE Reaches Capitol Hill."

10. Matt Loffman. "What's Driving the Movement to Abolish ICE?" *PBS*, 6 July 2018, pbs.org. Accessed 28 July 2020.

11. Loffman, "What's Driving the Movement to Abolish ICE?"

12. "Inhofe Joins GOP Senators in Introducing Resolution to Support ICE." *James M. Inhofe*, 11 July 2018, inhofe.senate.gov. Accessed 28 July 2020.

CHAPTER 9. WHAT HAPPENS NEXT?

1. Jynnah Radford and Luis Noe-Bustamante. "Facts on U.S. Immigrants, 2017." *Pew Research Center*, 3 June 2019, pewresearch.org. Accessed 28 July 2020.

2. Leanna Garfield, Shayanne Gal, and Andy Kiersz. "Migrant Detention Centers in the US Are Under Fire for Their 'Horrifying' Conditions—and There's at Least One in Every State. This Map Shows Which Have the Most." *Business Insider*, 5 July 2019, businessinsider.com. Accessed 28 July 2020.

3. "U.S. Immigration and Customs Enforcement Fiscal Year 2019 Enforcement and Removal Operations Report." *US ICE*, 2019, ice.gov. Accessed 28 July 2020.

4. "U.S. Immigration and Customs Enforcement Fiscal Year 2019."

5. Elaine Kamarck and Christine Stenglein. "How Many Undocumented Immigrants Are in the United States and Who Are They?" *Policy 2020 Brookings*, 12 Nov. 2019, brookings.edu. Accessed 28 July 2020.

6. "ICE and DOJ Return Christopher Columbus Letter to Spain." *US ICE*, 6 June 2018, ice.gov. Accessed 28 July 2020.

7. Katie Shepherd. "Government Quietly Increases ICE Detention to 48,000 Beds During the Shutdown." *Immigration Impact*, 31 Jan. 2019, immigrationimpact.com. Accessed 28 July 2020.

8. "U.S. Immigration and Customs Enforcement Fiscal Year 2019."

9. "Stepped Up Illegal-Entry Prosecutions Reduce Those for Other Crimes." *TRAC Immigration*, 6 Aug. 2018, trac.syr.edu. Accessed 28 July 2020.

10. "DNC Keynote: American Dream Is Not a Sprint." *Chicago Tribune*, 4 Sept. 2012, chicagotribune.com. Accessed 28 July 2020.

INDEX

ABOUT THE
AUTHOR

CYNTHIA KENNEDY HENZEL

Cynthia Kennedy Henzel has a bachelor's degree in social studies education and a master's in geography. She has worked as a teacher-educator in many countries. Currently, she writes books and develops educational materials for social studies, history, science, and ELL students. She has written more than 90 books for young people.

ABOUT THE CONSULTANT

LUIS F. JIMÉNEZ

Luis F. Jiménez is an associate professor in the political science department at the University of Massachusetts Boston. His main research interests are Latin American politics, immigration, and US-Latin American relations. He has published in *PS: Political Science and Politics* and in *Social Science Quarterly*. In addition, he has published a book with the University Press of Florida on the impact that Latin American migrants have in their home countries.